Pearlie in Paris

WENDY HARMER

Illustrated by Gypsy Taylor

RANDOM HOUSE AUSTRALIA

For Mlle Claudia, the fashionista!

A Random House book
Published by Random House Australia Pty Ltd
Level 3, 100 Pacific Highway, North Sydney NSW 2060
www.randomhouse.com.au

First published by Random House Australia in 2011
Copyright © Out of Harms Way Pty Ltd 2011

Addresses for companies within the Random House Group can be found
at www.randomhouse.com.au/offices.

National Library of Australia
  Cataloguing-in-Publication Entry

Harmer, Wendy
Pearlie in Paris / written by Wendy Harmer; illustrated by Gypsy Taylor
ISBN 978 1 74166 380 8 (pbk.)
Series: Harmer, Wendy. Pearlie the park fairy; 14
Target audience: For primary school age
Subjects: Fairies – Juvenile fiction
          Paris (France) – Juvenile fiction
Other authors/contributors: Taylor, Gypsy

A823.4

Designed and typeset by Jobi Murphy
Printed and bound by Everbest Printing Co.Ltd, China
10 9 8 7 6 5 4 3 2 1

It was springtime in Paris! From high on Queen Emerald's magic ladybird, Pearlie could see many grand buildings, the Eiffel Tower, and beautiful parks bursting with fresh flowers.

'Hurly-burly!' sang Pearlie. She was thrilled to be visiting one of the world's loveliest cities when it was at its prettiest.

'There's the *Jardin du Palais Royal*!' she called to the ladybird. 'That's where Fifi the Fairy lives. In a palace! Imagine that!'

The ladybird darted through the royal grounds, the magnificent gardens and set Pearlie down in a bed of bright yellow and pink tulips.

From behind a bloom, out jumped a small fairy.

She tapped one tiny toe.

'*Enfin!*' she said in a cross voice. 'At last!'

Pearlie smiled and said, 'Hello, my name is –'

'You do not speak French?' asked the fairy.

'No, I'm afraid not,' Pearlie replied.

'*Zut alors!*' muttered the fairy. 'You are late and you do not speak French. This is too, too bad! It is just as well that you are very pretty. Follow me. *Tout de suite!*'

The little fairy zoomed away. 'That means "at once"!' she called over her shoulder.

The fairy flitted along a palace terrace and then landed in front of a small door at the foot of a grand stone staircase.

Pearlie quickly followed. She wondered if this could be the famous Fifi? She wasn't very friendly.

Once inside, Pearlie was amazed to see a long hall lit by splendid crystal chandeliers.

'Twirlyswirly,' sighed Pearlie. 'How beautiful.'

The little fairy handed Pearlie a lovely ruffled gown.

'Take off those plain clothes and old boots and put this on *immediatement*!' she ordered. 'My other models are already dressed.'

How rude, thought Pearlie. Her own dress was pretty enough and her boots were almost brand new.

'There must be some mistake,' she said. 'I'm not a model.'

'But why not?' said the fairy. 'Your hair is *magnifique!*'

'Why, thank you very much,' Pearlie blushed.
'But, may I ask, are you Fifi?'

'*Oui!*' said the fairy as she smoothed her dark
hair. 'The most famous fairy in all of Paris!'

'Well, I'm Pearlie the Park Fairy and I've come to
visit from Jubilee Park.'

une

'Oh, *excuse moi*!' exclaimed Fifi. She then kissed Pearlie, not once, but three times, as the French like to do. 'I forgot you were coming! You see, I have been so busy with my spring collection.'

Pearlie wasn't exactly sure what a 'spring collection' was, although she knew it wasn't like the cake crumbs the ants collected from picnics on the sunny lawns of Jubilee Park.

Fifi opened a wardrobe. Inside were many more fabulous shimmering gowns.

'It is my fashion for the new season. I sew them from the petals of French lilies, roses, iris and sprigs of rosemary,' said Fifi proudly.

'I make my own clothes, too,' said Pearlie. 'I have some here in my bag. Would you like to see them?'

'Er ... *non*,' Fifi sniffed. 'No time. You will have a little tea and a sweet cake and then I will show you how clothes are *properly* made in *belle Paris*.'

Soon Pearlie was sitting in a fancy chair sipping a delicious cup of rosehip tea and nibbling on an almond macaron.

'You will be truly amazed,' said Fifi. She clapped her hands and from a doorway came tall and lovely fairies who paraded up and down the carpet, one by one.

They wore long glittering gowns, flowing capes and the most extraordinary feathered hats. Their dainty high-heeled slippers were covered with tiny jewels.

Pearlie *was* amazed. 'Stitches and sequins!' she gasped.

They were hardly the sort of clothes Pearlie would wear to work in Jubilee Park when she was hanging dewdrops in the spider webs.

It was late when the parade finished and Fifi showed Pearlie to her charming *boudoir*. (That's the French word for a lady's bedroom.)

'Sleep well,' said Fifi. 'Tomorrow everyone is coming for the parade and it will be a very busy day. *Bonsoir*. Goodnight.'

Under the stairs of the Palais Royal, Pearlie slept soundly.

At dawn she was woken by a terrible shout.

EeeeEEEK!! *oh non, non, non !!!*

Pearlie flew out of bed and found Fifi on the floor in front of her wardrobe. Her beautiful clothes were now little more than scraps of leaves, petals and a few feathers and sequins. The sad pile was covered in silver slime.

'Roots and twigs!' said Pearlie. 'What happened?'

'Someone left my front door open last night and all my beautiful clothes – *toutes mes belles robes* – have been EATEN!' Fifi cried.

'Who would do such a thing?' asked Pearlie.

'It is the work of *escargot*! SNAILS!' Fifi threw
herself into a chair and wept loudly. 'All the
fine fairies of Paris will soon be here to see my
collection! What will I have to show for all my
hard work? *C'est un catastrophe!*' she cried.

Pearlie knew that if there were no clothes
for the fashion parade, the day would indeed
be a catastrophe.

Poor Fifi, thought Pearlie.

She immediately set to work and followed
the silver snail trail out the door and through
the tulip beds.

'AARGH! GROAN!'

The sound was being made by a fat snail, who was looking very unhappy.

He was the guilty one, all right! In fact, he still had a bit of sleeve hanging out of his mouth.

'Aha!' said Pearlie. 'I hope you had a fine feast, you greedy thing.'

'OOOH!' moaned the snail.

Pearlie felt sorry for him. He really did not look well.

'Can I get you something? I'm Pearlie, what's your name?' she said, hoping he spoke English.

'Percy,' he replied. 'EERGH! A small cup of water, if you please.'

Pearlie fetched the water and when Percy had drunk it, he felt up to telling his tale.

'Two days ago I came from my home in London across the English Channel by mistake in a box of spinach,' he said sadly. 'When the vegetables were delivered to the palace kitchen, I spied the chef. Do you know they EAT snails in Paris? They serve us with garlic butter!'

'Hurly-burly!' said Pearlie. 'How dreadful!'

'I was lucky to make my escape,' Percy said with a shudder.

'So what happened last night?' Pearlie asked.

'I was lost and wandering the garden when I smelled a beautiful aroma. It was like a dream. I followed the scent and was soon having the most delicious dinner I have ever eaten, until something went down the wrong way.'

'I imagine it was a sequin,' sighed Pearlie. 'They're very hard to digest.'

'BURP! Yes they are,' said Percy.

Pearlie then informed Percy of exactly what he
had done. He had dined out on all of Fifi's finery.

'Good gracious,' he said. 'How truly ghastly
of me.'

Percy agreed to find Fifi and explain everything.

'*Je suis désolé*. I'm *so* sorry.' Percy felt so guilty he apologised to Fifi in French *and* English.

But Fifi was still mad.

'You can't blame him,' said Pearlie. 'Snails do have very poor eyesight.'

'Your spring collection was five stars!' said Percy.
'Apart from ... BURP!'

Up came a sequin which landed at Fifi's feet.

Fifi's face turned a dull shade of green. 'Eergh!
I make fashion, not fine food,' she wailed. 'What
will my models wear? I must show *something*!'

Then Pearlie had an idea.

'The models can borrow my new spring clothes!'
she said. 'They're made from wattle, lilly pilly and
kangaroo paw.'

Fifi wrinkled her tiny nose. 'You make your
clothes from the feet of *kangourou*? *Non!* This
will not do. Not at all.'

'No,' laughed Pearlie. 'They're all native
Australian flowers. I reckon no-one here has
ever seen them before.'

'Hmm,' said Fifi. 'That could be something very, very new. Show me what you have and perhaps I can make a quick alteration with a bow or a sequin ... *çà et là* ... here and there?'

Soon Pearlie and Fifi were sitting with their heads together and their sewing needles flashing.

Later that afternoon, the chandeliers sparkled on a glamorous gathering of the fashionista fairies of Paris. Some had flown in from London and New York!

They were looking forward to the delights Fifi had to offer.

Pearlie sprinkled fairy dust perfumed with spring flowers from back home in Jubilee Park.

'Ooh, la, la!' the fairies exclaimed.

Percy appeared as the Snail of Ceremonies.
(After all, he spoke two languages.)

'*Mesdames et Messieurs*, Ladies and Gentlemen,'
he said. '*Bienvenue!* Welcome!'

The lights dimmed and the show began. Fifi was
very nervous, but Pearlie held her hand tightly.

It was a dazzling parade!

The crowd went wild to see bright fluffy balls of yellow wattle, purple lilly pilly berries, the blazing red of desert flowers and the glowing colours of the kangaroo paw.

All of Pearlie's dresses had been given that special 'Fifi' touch and looked *magnifique*!

When the lights came up, the audience stood and clapped wildly.

'*Superb! Extraordinaire! Awesome!*' they cheered.

Fifi and Pearlie took a bow together and kissed one another's cheeks – not once, twice, three, but *four* times.

'*Merci*, Pearlie. Thank you,' said Fifi. 'With your help, once again I am the toast of Paris. You and Monsieur Snail are to be my guests here at the Palais Royal for as long as you would like.'

Pearlie and Percy had an excellent time seeing all the sights. Pearlie flew to the top of the Eiffel Tower and Percy slid all the way up (which, it must be admitted, did take a week, but Pearlie didn't mind).

When spring was over it was time for Pearlie to leave, although Percy wanted to stay forever. Fifi said he was very welcome to stay and that she would make sure he wasn't eaten for supper.

Pearlie was sad to leave Paris but she was delighted with the lovely gowns Fifi gave her.

She could just imagine herself fluttering though Jubilee Park at dawn, glittering in French sequins from the top of her feathery hat to the toes of her jewelled slippers.

'I'll always remember Paris in the springtime,' she sighed.

'*Au revoir*,' Pearlie called softly. 'Goodbye!'